My Spectacular Self

Tiger's Tough Time

A Story About Managing Emotions

by Rosario Martinez

illustrated by Román Díaz

PICTURE WINDOW BOOKS
a capstone imprint

For you, little one —R.M.

Published by Picture Window Books, an imprint of Capstone
1710 Roe Crest Drive, North Mankato, Minnesota 56003
capstonepub.com

Library of Congress Cataloging-in-Publication Data is available
on the Library of Congress website.
ISBN: 9781666340181 (hardcover)
ISBN: 9781666340228 (paperback)
ISBN: 9781666340358 (ebook PDF)

Summary: When Wyatt the tiger gets frustrated, nervous, or mad, he makes sure everyone around him knows about it. Sometimes he whines. Sometimes he cries. And sometimes he even yells. Can his friends show him how to manage his emotions and share his feelings in a better way?

Special thanks to Amber Chandler for her consulting work.

Designed by Hilary Wacholz

Meet Wyatt

HOBBIES: climbing trees, playing ball with friends, and collecting buttons

FAVORITE BOOKS: *Ultimate Frisbee* and *Big Reflections in the Water*

FAVORITE FOOD: sandwiches, blueberries, and beetles

FUTURE GOALS: be an archaeologist, someone who studies ancient cultures and artifacts

GOALS FOR THIS YEAR

- ATTEND A MUSIC FESTIVAL

- GO CAMPING WITH FRIENDS

- BE IN A FRISBEE TOURNAMENT

- FIND MORE SHINY BUTTONS

Wyatt loved visiting and playing with his friends.
Especially on days when they met at Antelope's house!

But sometimes, everything bothered Wyatt.

Throw it here, Wyatt!

"It's okay. The rain won't last long," Toucan said.

But an uneasy feeling fluttered in Wyatt's stomach.
He was disappointed the rain was ruining everything.

"What are we going to play now?" Wyatt asked.

"We're going to play lots of games inside," Antelope said.

Frustrated, Wyatt threw the Frisbee so fast it ZOOMED into a treetop.

He stomped his foot.

"We can after the rain passes," Toucan said.

Wyatt frowned. "But I don't want to wait."

Inside, Antelope said, "Let's play musical chairs!"

The music started, and the animal friends marched around the chairs.

They circled the chairs—one round, two rounds, three rounds—before the music stopped.

When the music stopped, only Wyatt was left without a chair.
He quickly tried to squeeze back into one.

Wyatt tightened his paws, and his whole body felt hot. He was so angry, he wanted to cry. "That's my chair! Toucan took my chair!"

"That's not very nice!" Zebra said.

Nothing was going right, and Wyatt's big feelings kept getting in the way. His friends were upset that he ruined the game. And Wyatt was worried they wouldn't want to play with him anymore.

"Maybe you can join us later," said Antelope.

Wyatt needed a break.

Despite his big feelings, Wyatt wanted to play. He walked quietly into the den to talk to Toucan.

"I'm sorry I tried to take your chair," Wyatt said. "I was just so mad that I didn't have one."

"I understand. You just wanted to keep playing," Toucan said.

"Can I play the next game?" Wyatt asked.

"Yes, we're playing statues! Just try not to move when the timer rings, or you'll lose!" Toucan said.

Once the timer rang, the animals stopped in place. Everyone made funny faces! Wyatt tried not to move—or laugh. But it was so hard!

Wyatt's face turned red. He was so frustrated.
He tried to stay calm, but . . .

"I used to get really upset sometimes too," Toucan said. "But I learned a way to calm myself down. I breathe in, ease my shoulders back, breathe out, and shake about."

"I don't think that will work," Wyatt growled. "I just need to go home."

"Just try it!" his friends insisted.

Wyatt was nervous, but he stepped into the middle of the room. He looked at his friends again. His body tensed, his paws were sweaty, and his face felt a little red.

But with a swish of his tail and his arms held beside him, Wyatt said, "Breathe in, ease my shoulders back, breathe out, and shake about."

Wyatt felt his body relax when he took a breath.

He felt even better when he
moved his shoulders back.

He breathed away the uneasy feelings that made him nervous and cranky.

Now that Wyatt had learned how to calm himself down, he didn't feel like he needed to go home. He was finally having fun.

"Wyatt, do you want to play another game?" asked Zebra.

Wyatt thought for a moment. He liked the sound of that!

Practice Managing Your Emotions

Our emotions—the way we feel—can overwhelm us sometimes, but that's okay! There are ways to manage our emotions that will help us feel better.

To manage your emotions . . .

pause and think about how you're feeling

take a deep breath, then let it out really loud

say how you feel out loud

use your favorite colors to draw a picture

sing your favorite song

Managing My Emotions Matters

1. It's important to talk about our emotions and share how we feel. Do you remember a time when you were feeling a lot of emotions? Describe how you felt.

2. Often our emotions can overwhelm us. Then we might get angry or break a rule. What are some things you can do to manage your feelings instead?

3. When you're feeling overwhelmed, take a moment to think about how you feel. Can you name the emotions you feel?

4. Telling others how we feel can help. How do you share your feelings with others?

5. Wyatt's behavior made playtime less fun for everyone. Can you think of a time when your emotions affected others? How did you manage your emotions? Would you change how you reacted?

About the Author

Rosario Martinez is a Mexican-American author. She was born in Monterrey, Nuevo Leon, Mexico, and raised in Dallas, Texas. Her love for stories and books was motivated from an early age by her grandmother's storytelling. She attended the University of Texas at Dallas, where she double majored in psychology and child learning and development. As an English as a second language speaker, she is a supporter of early literacy and access to literature, and believes everyone deserves a place in the pages of a book. She lives in Dallas with her partner and four sweet, but demanding, cats. Visit her at rosariomartinezwrites.com.

About the Illustrator

Román Díaz was born in Mexico. Since he was a child, he always wanted to draw like adults. Now that he is an adult, he likes to draw like children. He's created illustrations for books, video games, and many other projects. He likes to eat colorful fruits and vegetables and admires animals in documentaries because it seems they have superpowers.